Alice Baburek

Silent Wings

Alice Baburek

# Silent Wings

## A Romantic Journey through Time

JustFiction Edition

**Impressum/Imprint (nur für Deutschland/only for Germany)**
Bibliografische Information der Deutschen Nationalbibliothek: Die Deutsche Nationalbibliothek verzeichnet diese Publikation in der Deutschen Nationalbibliografie; detaillierte bibliografische Daten sind im Internet über http://dnb.d-nb.de abrufbar.
Alle in diesem Buch genannten Marken und Produktnamen unterliegen warenzeichen-, marken- oder patentrechtlichem Schutz bzw. sind Warenzeichen oder eingetragene Warenzeichen der jeweiligen Inhaber. Die Wiedergabe von Marken, Produktnamen, Gebrauchsnamen, Handelsnamen, Warenbezeichnungen u.s.w. in diesem Werk berechtigt auch ohne besondere Kennzeichnung nicht zu der Annahme, dass solche Namen im Sinne der Warenzeichen- und Markenschutzgesetzgebung als frei zu betrachten wären und daher von jedermann benutzt werden dürften.

Coverbild: www.ingimage.com

Verlag: JustFiction! Edition ist ein Imprint der
LAP LAMBERT Academic Publishing GmbH & Co. KG
Heinrich-Böcking-Str. 6-8, 66121 Saarbrücken, Deutschland
Telefon +49 681 37 20 310, Telefax +49 681 37 20 310-9
Email: info@justfiction-edition.com

Herstellung in Deutschland:
Schaltungsdienst Lange o.H.G., Berlin
Books on Demand GmbH, Norderstedt
Reha GmbH, Saarbrücken
Amazon Distribution GmbH, Leipzig
ISBN: 978-3-8454-4556-4

**Imprint (only for USA, GB)**
Bibliographic information published by the Deutsche Nationalbibliothek: The Deutsche Nationalbibliothek lists this publication in the Deutsche Nationalbibliografie; detailed bibliographic data are available in the Internet at http://dnb.d-nb.de.
Any brand names and product names mentioned in this book are subject to trademark, brand or patent protection and are trademarks or registered trademarks of their respective holders. The use of brand names, product names, common names, trade names, product descriptions etc. even without a particular marking in this works is in no way to be construed to mean that such names may be regarded as unrestricted in respect of trademark and brand protection legislation and could thus be used by anyone.

Cover image: www.ingimage.com

Publisher: JustFiction! Edition
is an imprint of the publishing house
LAP LAMBERT Academic Publishing GmbH & Co. KG
Heinrich-Böcking-Str. 6-8, 66121 Saarbrücken, Germany
Phone +49 681 37 20 310, Fax +49 681 37 20 310-9
Email: info@justfiction-edition.com

Printed in the U.S.A.
Printed in the U.K. by (see last page)
ISBN: 978-3-8454-4556-4

# SILENT WINGS

by Alice Baburek

To my dear parents who have left this world too soon.
You will always be remembered and loved by your family.

# Acknowledgements

I would like to acknowledge all of my supporters of my writing endeavors. A sincere "thank you" from the bottom of my heart.

# Chapter 1

Days for Margaret Livingston dragged by since the death of her husband, Charlie. Her children, grown with families of their own, had long forgotten about their ailing mother. Where had she gone wrong? Wrapped up inside their own worlds, leaving Margaret to live out the remainder of her days alone, holding onto precious memories of her beloved Charlie to keep her alive.

The old, lonely woman lay silently awake on the lumpy mattress. She blinked back the tears as she outstretched her aching arm to the empty side of the bed. She struggled a minute or two before she painfully lifted, then turned her aged, decrepit body. It had been many years since Charlie snuggled close to her side. The faint smell of his Old Spice aftershave used to linger on her nightgown for days. She couldn't wait for each night when his muscular arms would hold her tight, calming her fears and leaving her with a sense of peace and tranquility.

Margaret sobbed against the worn and tattered pillowcase. The crippling arthritis held her captive—not only in mind and body, but soul. An overwhelming stench of medicinal remedies hung heavy in the air. It permeated the dingy walls of her dark and dreary bedroom. The discolored venation blinds remained closed, sealing out the penetrating early morning light.

As minutes turned into hours, her flattened stomach grumbled from the devouring emptiness. Margaret forced herself to dress. A slight shiver ran down her deteriorated, curved spine. Arduously, she pulled the oversized wool sweater on to keep warm. She took a deep breath before reaching clumsily for the metal walker. She hesitated a brief moment. With great difficulty, she tried to focus on the image which sat upon the red-stained dresser next to her bed. A tiny smile curled from her wrinkled lips. Margaret reached for the old photo and held it close. The picture had yellowed over the years, but the handsome and dashing uniformed young flyer remained ageless; next to him stood a beautiful, vibrant woman lovingly at his side.

"Charlie," she whispered. Her heart filled with sorrow. Margaret closed her weary eyes. It seemed like only yesterday when they had first met. She let her mind drift back—back to those wonderful days—she could still see him now, standing tall and proud dressed in his olive-drab uniform.

"May I help?" questioned Akio Takahashi, the owner of Sunshine Dry Cleaners. Charlie Livingston smiled. A service dress jacket draped over his arm. He pointed to the missing button.

"Yes. I need a button sewn onto my jacket. I'm kind of in a hurry. How long will it take?" His voice was smooth and casual. The brown-black hair on top his head was clipped close. Margaret Whitmore peeked out from behind the hanging garments. Her eyes focused on the handsome man in uniform. Her flowered cotton dress stuck heavy to her sweaty skin. She had been sewing and steaming clothes for hours in the back room. Margaret listened with extreme interest as the two men conversed.

"You fight in war?" asked Akio in broken English.

Lt. Livingston slowly nodded his head.

"You pilot?" persisted the inquisitive shop-keeper.

Charlie chuckled, then sighed. "Yes, I'm a pilot for the US Army Air Force."

"How long flying?" asked Takahashi.

"You're just full of questions, aren't you? Well, since the beginning of the war. Now, how about fixing my button?" pleaded Charlie.

Akio's eyes narrowed. He let out a huge sigh. "My helper will do for you," he stated.

Margaret's face blushed instantly. She knew it was up to her to fix his jacket. Lt. Livingston diverted his attention to the young, attractive woman hidden amongst the clothes.

"Come out, child! Work to do, now!" Akio commanded, then swiftly walked away.

Margaret gently pushed past the hanging clothes and moved gracefully to the counter, while trying desperately to smooth her wrinkled dress. "May I help you, sir?" she asked in a timid voice. Her heart pounded in her ears. His blue eyes were breathtaking, and held Margaret captive.

Charlie's smile stretched from ear to ear. Pearly white teeth gleamed in the dim light.

"Well, by all means, and yes, you may help me, Miss…" he said, purposely leaving the sentence unfinished.

"Whitmore, Margaret Whitmore. My name is Margaret Whitmore," she lightly replied. She slowly placed a few strands of damp hair behind her ear.

"Miss Whitmore, if I may be so bold, you have the loveliest brown eyes I have ever seen!" he exclaimed. Charlie's eyes glazed with pleasure. Margaret's cheeks flushed with embarrassment. Suddenly, Akio returned, breaking the spell.

"No time for talky!" shouted Akio from across the room. "I pay you to work, work, work!" Both Charlie and Margaret began to laugh. The butterflies that raced within her stomach eased.

"He's quite demanding, isn't he?" commented Charlie.

Margaret shook her head in disagreement. "No, not really, I mean Mr. Takahashi is really a sweet old man. I think the reason he was asking you questions about being a pilot is because he's quite upset over the attack on Pearl Harbor. He's from Japan. He said Japan dishonored their ancestry," said Margaret. "He's ashamed of what they did." Charlie listened with extreme interest. "May I ask you a question?" Margaret's voice was low.

"Yes, surely you may, Miss Whitmore," he said.

"If you can't give me an answer, I understand. Do you know why Mr. Takahashi had to register with the U.S. government?" she questioned.

Charlie remained silent for a brief moment. "Let me try and explain. A direct order was passed down directly from President Roosevelt. I was told that the President, along with other high-ranking officials, thought long and hard before taking such drastic action. They believed that the Japanese-Americans could become a security threat to this great nation." Charlie hesitated then realized how silly it must have sounded.

"Mr. Takahashi…a threat to our country?" Margaret let out a huge sigh. "How could this be?"

"I'm sure it's just a precaution, and nothing will become of it," consoled Charlie.

"I hope you're right…Mister…" Margaret's voice trailed away.

"Let me apologize for my lack of manners. I am Lt. Charlie Livingston, at your service, Miss Whitmore," he announced. Charlie bent slightly at the waist. Margaret giggled like an infatuated schoolgirl.

"If you want to stop back before we close, say in about an hour? I'll have the button sewn on for you, Lt. Charlie Livingston!" exclaimed Margaret. She felt an instant attraction to the charming soldier.

"I will gladly return within the hour, Miss Whitmore. I look forward to when we meet again," he said.

She could feel his gaze linger upon her face. "Please, do call me Margaret," she eagerly replied.

"Agreed, as long as you call me, Charlie!" And with that said, he turned on his heel and left Margaret alone to do her job.

Akio Takahashi had left early, leaving Margaret behind to close-up shop. Margaret looked out the window with anticipation. Sewing on a button took only a few minutes. She held the jacket close to her face. She couldn't believe the butterflies, once again, rambling around inside as she thought about the handsome Lt. Charlie Livingston. No man had seemed to merit a second glance—until now. Suddenly, the shop bell clanged. The door opened wide. Instantly, she pulled the jacket away and stood up to greet him.

"Good evening, Margaret." Charlie gave a slight bow. His manly features beamed with delight, his movements smooth and deliberate.

"Good evening to you, Charlie." Margaret held up his dress service jacket. The missing button had been professionally replaced.

"I'm truly impressed by your unique skills," retorted Charlie. He examined his coat.

"It's nothing," said Margaret shyly. "Sewing on a button is one of the easiest alterations for a seamstress or, for that matter, anyone!"

"Oh, but I beg to differ, Margaret. You see, I may be able to pilot a plane through enemy lines, but for the life of me, I cannot sew a button on my own coat," he said in all honesty.

"Did you not have to learn this womanly skill in the service?" she questioned. "Keeping your uniform intact is not a requirement? Something learned by all service men?"

"Indeed, you are correct, Margaret. But my sewing competency falls extremely short of completing the mission," he jested.

Margaret felt unusually comfortable with Charlie. Just then, he began to fish inside his pants pocket. "Oh no, Charlie, it was my honor to serve an American soldier. It's the least I can do during this awful time of war."

For a brief moment, neither one spoke. They locked longingly onto one another's eyes.

"May I have the pleasure of escorting you home, Margaret Whitmore?" Charlie cleared his dry throat.

"I would be delighted, Lt. Charlie Livingston." And with that said, Margaret locked up the door to Sunshine Dry Cleaners, and started down a new road in her life with Charlie Livingston.

As the reality of the present seeped back into her mind, tears overflowed onto Margaret's sunken cheeks. She glanced over at the other faded photo. Her two children, Jessie and Jane, smiled back. Why did they not come and visit their mother? It had been several years since either one of them had set foot inside her crumbling home. Suddenly, Margaret's gnarled fingers began to tremble and shake. The timeless photograph of Charlie fell helplessly from within her unstable grasp, only to shatter into tiny pieces upon the dirty floor.

.      "No!" she cried out in desperation. Shards of cutting glass bounced playfully about, then quietly remained still. There, in the middle of the rubble, untouched and intact, was the only physical proof of her dwindling memories. Margaret sighed, and then chuckled with relief.

"Maybe with a little luck…" Her words trailed away. Without giving it any thought, she foolishly tried to retrieve her last tangible connection to the past.

"Oh my!" cried Margaret in vain. She struggled desperately to keep upright. Her wasted and weakened body collapsed. She tumbled dangerously off the side of the bed. Within a matter of a second, Margaret's head viciously struck the worn-out night stand. Dizziness and nausea consumed her as she tumbled helplessly to the floor. Visions darted across her confused mind— meshed together images of Charlie, then Jessie and Jane. Then out of sheer desperation, she had nothing left to do but to succumb to the deep state of unconsciousness which lured her mind back into the past…

"What will you do now that Sunshine Dry Cleaners is soon to close its doors?" asked Charlie. The wrinkles between his brows deepened. Margaret hung her head low.

"I don't know. I can't believe Mr. Takahashi is being sent to a concentration camp. It's just not fair! He has nothing to do with the war! That poor man came to America to find a better way of life. All the sweat and work he put into his shop…!" she sobbed.

Charlie knew he was falling deeper in love with Margaret. He held her lovingly against his broad chest. With gentleness he tried to soothe her fears. "I'm sure he'll be just fine, Margaret. There are many others like Akio Takahashi. Once the war is over, he'll be able to return to his home and continue on with business as usual. But in the meantime, what are your plans, Margaret?" And before she could answer through her dwindling sniffles, he tenderly wiped away her tears with his clean, white handkerchief.

"Margaret, I know we have only been seeing one another for a little over a year, but my heart is bursting. I can no longer ignore the heart-filled love I hold deep inside for you." Margaret was stunned by Charlie's abruptness to such a delicate subject.

"I have a confession to make, Margaret Whitmore. I love you more than life itself, and… Margaret Whitmore, will you marry me and be my wife?" he proposed.

Margaret remained silent for a moment. He waited nervously for an answer. She smiled bashfully and placed her hand on his shoulder. "Charlie Livingston…there is nothing in this world I could want more than to be your bride."

Filled with hope and promise, Charlie encircled her waist. With precision he lifted her high up into the air shouting with delight. "You've made me the happiest man on earth!" Charlie spun her around and around. Then, as quickly as he started, he abruptly stopped.

"Wait! I forgot…how foolish and inconsiderate of me!" he mumbled. Charlie dug deep inside the pocket of his uniform. Margaret gave him a wide-eyed look. In the palm of his hand, lay a diamond ring. "Margaret Whitmore, will you marry me?" asked Charlie once again. But this time, he slipped the thin ring onto her shaky finger.

Margaret gave a teary smile. "Yes!" she whispered. And as their eyes locked onto one another, he eagerly leaned in and kissed her warm and inviting lips. After a few seconds, he reluctantly let go. His radiating smile had vanished.

"What is it, Charlie?"Margaret asked. She lightly caressed his smooth-shaven face with her petite finger. For a brief second, she thought he had doubts about the proposal.

He closed his eyes, and then lowered his head. "My orders came in, Margaret. I am to fly out early tomorrow morning, and…I don't know how long I will be gone this time." Charlie could not bear to look into her sorrowful eyes.

Margaret turned about and covered her face with trembling hands. "I will wait for you, Charlie!" Her tiny voice cracked with streaming emotions. She stared down at the tiny diamond on her finger through blurry eyes.

Charlie rushed to his fiancée's side. "Oh, my darling, there is nothing I would want more than to come back and be your husband. I promise you, Margaret, when I return, we will marry and live as husband and wife for the rest of our lives." Margaret, filled with despair, threw her arms around his muscular neck and held on with all her might. For a brief moment, neither one dared to say a word to break this magical spell.

"Where is the Air Force sending you this time?" she murmured. She nuzzled against his silky neck, her eyes wet with tears.

Charlie knew he could not answer. His missions were always classified top secret. He had been entrusted with one of the most closely guarded military secrets during World War II. He was bound to protect these secrets, even if it meant with his life.

"Now, Margaret, you know I cannot reveal vital military information. Please, don't ask me to betray my oath of silence," he whispered in her ear.

Margaret prayed that Charlie would keep his word and come back to her alive. "I don't want to let you go!" she cried. She held onto him even tighter.

He closed his eyes and took a deep breath, ingesting the faint smell of palm oil that lingered in her soft, curly hair. "I promise to write you with each and every spare moment I am given, my love."

And then, he tenderly kissed her tear-soaked lips one last time. Margaret had never felt so alone in her entire life as she did at that very moment.

# Chapter 2

The night air had become brisk and found its way inside her full-length wool coat. Margaret shivered slightly as she climbed the wooden steps. She shifted the small bag of groceries to open the back door. Once inside the warm kitchen, she set the bag upon the round table. She laid her coat across the back of the chair. It didn't take long before the soup cans and box of crackers were put away.

"Is that you, Margaret?" cried a voice. Margaret turned the knob under the tin kettle.

"Yes, it's me; you should be in bed resting, Father."

His head hung slightly to the side as he slipped into an uncontrollable coughing fit. Margaret rushed to her father's side. The clean white handkerchief turned bright red.

"Did you want me to call Dr. Clark?" she asked with concern. Margaret knelt by the recliner. His head fell back against the cushioned chair. He gasped for air.

"And what do you really think the good doctor could possibly do to help me now?" His voice was raspy. Grasping at his chest, he desperately fought to catch his breath. For the longest time, Margaret refused to face the inevitable truth. Eric Whitmore was dying. Each day was a blessing for Margaret, but a living hell for her father. So many nights, she prayed for his suffering to stop, yet in the back of her mind, she couldn't bear the thought of losing him. But Margaret could no longer deny his inescapable fate—his courageous fight to live was abruptly coming to an end. Tears swelled in her eyes as she gazed upon the decrepit old man. Eric placed his trembling, oversized hand on top of Margaret's, then gently squeezed.

"Margaret, you've been my guardian angel since I became ill, but I've grown so weak and tired. Please...please, Margaret, you must let me go," he whispered. "I know it's a hard decision to make," he coughed again and again, "but stay strong, Margaret." Blood oozed from his thin lips. "Know that I will always love you." Agonizing pain soared through his tired, depleted lungs.

"Daddy, I can't let go...please try to hold on! I'll call Dr. Clark!" she cried. Margaret frantically wiped the tears away from her burning eyes. As she dashed to the phone on the end table, the ailing man gave one last horrible wail.

"No!" she screamed. But it was too late. Instantly, she rushed to his side. Margaret's prayers had finally been answered as her dying father succumbed to his terminal illness. She knew how he had suffered each and every day, but a little bit of selfishness surfaced in wanting her father to live on. And as the heavens above called out his name, Eric Whitmore left this life, leaving behind a decayed, empty shell and a loving daughter.

The funeral was plain and simple. Eric Whitmore was dressed in his best suit. A handful of neighbors and friends gathered together inside his living room to say their final farewells. At the end of the evening, Margaret stood alone by the side of her father's pine casket, and once again wept. Mental and physical exhaustion tugged at her weakened state of being. Margaret could fight it no more and collapsed on the sofa. There she would find no peace, only a restless sleep filled with darkened images of the father she had loved and lost.

The bitter cold wind rustled a few remaining leaves around the headstones. Margaret felt numb as Father O'Brien escorted her back to an empty house. He had been a good friend to her father for nearly twenty-five years. And when Eric became bedridden, it was Father O'Brien who made the special effort to visit him more often than not.

"Margaret, I want you to know I'm here if you ever feel the need to talk to someone," commented Father O'Brien. Margaret hung her head low. She looked about the silent house, and wondered what would become of her now. Loneliness crept into her soul with the loss of her father and her fiancé, Charlie, at bay.

"Margaret, are you alright?" he asked.

Margaret forced a weak smile. "Yes, and thank you, Father O'Brien; I wouldn't have been able to get through any of this without your kindness and continual support."

Father O'Brien touched his wide-brimmed hat and gave a slight nod. "You know where to find me, if you should need me, Margaret. God be with you, my child." And with that said, Father O'Brien left Margaret to grieve for herself as the last remaining person alive with the Whitmore name.

# Chapter 3

Margaret filled her days working long hours at the factory along with two hundred other women. Most of the men across the country had been sent off to war. For the first time in history, women filled these empty positions throughout the entire United States.

Letters from Charlie came few and far between. His letters were always short and sweet. Margaret continued to remain in the dark about his whereabouts. Then late September of 1942, communication from Charlie had suddenly ceased. Margaret's worse fears surfaced. She thought she had lost him forever. But she had to hear for herself about the fate of her loving husband-to-be, Charlie.

"Are you Mrs. Charlie Livingston?" asked the young officer at the Air Force Administration Office. The chaos inside the huge building was astonishing. Line after line of soldiers' wives waited to hear the unspeakable.

"Well…no, but I'm his fiancé, and I need to find out what happened to him…I need to know if he is still alive," she pleaded.

The uniformed soldier heaved a boring sigh and adjusted the stack of papers on his desk. "I'm sorry, Miss…but unless you can prove you're his wife, I am not authorized to release any confidential information regarding Lt. Charlie Livingston. May I help the next person in line?" he shouted, looking directly past Margaret.

"Wait! I'm not through...you don't understand!" she cried. The unseasoned airman stood up.

"Please, there are others who are waiting in line!" He motioned for her to leave. Margaret knew it was no use. She was getting nowhere fast. Regretfully, she stood up and left in despair.

As she made her way down the steps, a cheerful woman dressed in military-style clothing approached her.

"Did you ever think about flying a plane?" she asked. Baffled, Margaret looked at the piece of paper in the woman's hand.

"We need good women to join the Women's Airforce Service Pilots. Please, take a few minutes of your time to look over this information sheet. You too can be of great service to your country." With that said, the woman in uniform moved on with her stack of pamphlets. Margaret instantly thought of Charlie. Could she too become a pilot? Margaret became fascinated by the idea of flying a plane.

On the way back to the house, she stopped by the public library. Several articles had been written but there was one in particular that proved to be quite informative. It told about the Women's Airforce Service Pilots, also known as WASPs. How it had been established under the auspice of President Roosevelt to fill the obvious gaps of "manpower" during World War II. Male pilots were in high demand. With the continuation of the war, it had become evident that there were not enough male pilots to serve all the necessary roles—especially the duties entailing military transport. The missions of the WASPs were well defined. The article went on giving a brief overview of the WASPs specific. Margaret was fascinated to learn about duties involved.

Margaret's enthusiasm had magnified into an intense determination to become a member of the WASPs. Leaving her factory job, she consumed her time with becoming a WASP. Margaret's steadfast perseverance enabled her to excel and become one of the 1,900 women who were accepted for flight training at the Ellington Army Air Field in Houston, Texas. There she rigorously studied and trained, befitting as one of the top female pilots. Finally, after passing the same strenuous flight training requirements expected by male pilots, she earned her flying wings.

But even during those several grueling months of active training, Margaret still had not received a single letter from Charlie. With a heart full of sorrow, she fought back the urge to give in and accept the inevitable. She would not give up on his safe return.

As the war continued to tear apart the globe and shatter the world of hope, Margaret's successful missions, overtime, earned her notable recognitions and the attention of Major General Henry H. Arnold. Major General Arnold was a member of the elite War Department General Staff, and held the prestige position of Deputy Chief of Staff.

"Major General Arnold, it is an honor, sir..."

Major General Arnold smiled, then waved his hand in the air for Margaret to stop. "Margaret Whitmore, the United States Air Force appreciates the undying and continuous devotion and determination set forth by the Women's Airforce Service Pilots. Please, sit down, Miss Whitmore." He stood up and gestured to the chair in front of his desk.

Margaret felt a tad nervous. She quickly adjusted her formal dress jacket and skirt. Her standard-issued WASP beret and dress gloves lay neatly in her lap. She swallowed slowly, and sat perfectly attentive. The Major General's eyes darted instantly to her gold pilot wings displayed above her left pocket—something Margaret was indeed proud of. His head tilted to the other side. He glanced at the WASP insignia sewn on the right-hand side of her uniform.

"Miss Whitmore, your obvious dedication to the Women's Airforce Service Pilots and to your country has been duly noted. Within a short period of time, you have successfully completed more than one hundred assignments, many which you had volunteered for, regardless of the surrounding danger. Quite an impressive record, if I may say so myself." One-by-one, he slowly turned the sheets of paper on his desk. Margaret's palms were beginning to sweat.

"I see you don't handle compliments very well," he murmured. The General looked at her above the rim of his glasses. Margaret gave up a weak smile. Major General Arnold slowly closed the file.

"We need someone to fly the B-25 Mitchell over to the Bougainville Airfield. The Japanese forces are advancing and holding us back. We need to open a direct route to the Philippines." He suddenly stood up and turned to look out the window. An uncomfortable silence filled the air. Margaret did not say a word. She waited patiently for the General to continue.

"Lt. Charlie Livingston was on a very secretive mission to Japan, when his B-29 Super Fortress bomber was intercepted by a Japanese fighter. The pilot of the B-29 mistakenly took the Japanese plane for a British Mosquito. By the time he realized his error, it was too late. The

Mitsubishi G4M got behind and shot them down before they even had the slightest chance to retaliate."

Suddenly, Margaret felt numb. Each day, she tried desperately to prepare herself for the worst, and now that day had come. "Is he…" Margaret could not finish.

The General slowly turned. His face was filled with sympathy. "The B-29 went down somewhere in the vicinity of Hiroshima. We're not actually sure if any of the crew survived the crash."

Mixed emotions flared inside. Margaret's brows crunched in the middle. "Sir, wasn't that the bomber which carried the atomic bomb?" she questioned. The pounding in her ears grew louder to the point that she could barely hear the General's words.

The General rubbed the bottom of his chin. "Yes, but how would you know about that…never mind." He turned back around and faced the window once again.

"I don't understand. If the plane crashed, why didn't the bomb explode? And if it did explode, nothing in its path of destruction would have survived. Am I not correct, sir?" she persisted.

The Major General rocked slightly back and forth on the balls of his feet, then spun around to meet her moist eyes. "What I'm about to tell you, Miss Whitmore, is highly classified and must never leave this room. If it wasn't for the fact that Lt. Livingston is…well, that doesn't matter. Do we have an understanding?" he said. His jaw clenched.

"Yes, sir," replied Margaret. Her breathing quickened.

"Heat sensors picked up a fire. The entire plane landed and secured itself against the side of a mountain. As luck would have it, the bomb was found still intact within the belly of the plane. The pilot must have been able to maneuver it safely to the ground without causing detonation. Radio distress signals were ordered not to be used in a time of crisis. But a rescue mission has already been deployed, and successfully retrieved the bomb."

Visions of Charlie rushed through her mind. "I don't understand, sir…if the bomb was retrieved, where are the men?" she asked.

He cleared his voice before he spoke again. "The pilot and copilot were instantly killed during the landing. The other four members of the crew are still missing; this includes Lt. Livingston, Margaret." The words sunk deep and struck a nerve.

"Sir—"

"Margaret, we are in the middle of a world war. We are struggling to push back our enemies as we speak." The General glanced down at his desk. He could not face the distraught woman.

"Sir, so what you are saying, is that these men risked their lives for nothing, because you're too busy fighting a war to go back and look for them?" Margaret's frustration turned to anger. Suddenly, the General looked up. His eyes narrowed.

"They knew the risk they were taking when they volunteered for the mission. They will stay behind enemy lines until our troops reach the area. As you already know, our pilots are in short demand." Major General Arnold once again sat down at his desk.

"I will fly your plane to Bougainville Airfield, General, and then I'm going to look for my fiancé," she said firmly. Margaret knew deep in her heart Charlie was still alive.

"You will do no such thing, Miss Whitmore, or I will have you removed from duty," he threatened.

Margaret stood up to leave. "Is that all, Major General?" she asked curtly.

Major General Arnold eyed her suspiciously. "Yes, that is all, for now." Margaret saluted the General, then in a huff, turned to leave.

"Margaret!" he called out after her. "Don't be a fool; you haven't the resources. Charlie's a good man. He'll find his way home, but you may not."

"We'll see about that, General," she murmured. With that said, Margaret slowly closed the General's door.

# Chapter 4

Margaret pursued her obsession to find her fiancé, Charlie Livingston. She used every available contact, and then called in on favors. It wasn't long before she was standing inside the San Diego War Relocation Camp. Housed there were thousands of Japanese Americans who were forcibly relocated, due to their Japanese ancestry.

"It seems your papers are in order, Miss Whitmore," commented Major Daniel DeWitt. He glanced up at Margaret from behind his metal desk.

"It will take a few minutes to retrieve Akio Takahashi. Please have a seat while you are waiting, Miss Whitmore." The Major stood up and opened the door. He gave orders to a soldier outside in the hallway.

Margaret instantly sat down. She tried desperately inside to remain calm. The young officer seemed to be skeptical of Margaret's intentions. She smoothed her uniform as she shifted on the metal chair.

"So, if I may ask, what kind of knowledge could this Jap possibly have that would be of **any** interest to us?" he probed. Margaret was appalled by this soldier's inappropriate behavior. He smiled, then raised his left eyebrow. His eyes quickly scanned her body.

"Major, I cannot reveal what I do not know," she said. "My orders are to fly Mr. Takahashi back to base in Maine where he will be interrogated for top secret information about the Japanese military." She cleared her throat and stared hard at the Major.

His smile was devious, hands smooth and clean, never having to dig the trenches on the battlefield. "He used to be an owner of a dry cleaning place, for heaven's sake!" he chuckled. The Major leaned back in his chair. His hands clasped tight behind his head.

"What a perfect cover, if I may say so myself," she said in a low tone.

His smile vanished. Seconds later, Major DeWitt abruptly stood up to leave.

"We will have Akio Takahashi brought to you within the hour, Miss Whitmore. You may stay here and wait. If you will excuse me, I must tend to my work." Major DeWitt stormed from the office, leaving Margaret alone.

Without hesitation, she retrieved the fake orders from the top of the Major's desk and placed them back inside her briefcase. Sweat lined her brow. She never had been a good liar. But Margaret knew this time it was for a worthy cause. If the Major had any military intelligence, he would have known instantly she was lying. It wasn't long before the MPs escorted Akio Takahashi to Major DeWitt's office.

"Thank you for your promptness," commented Margaret. The two military guards followed them both out to the gates. Akio Takahashi did not say a word.

Finally, when they were free and safely off the base, Akio relaxed in his seat. "I knew someday you come," he whispered. His eyes were sad and heavy. His face had aged tremendously since his days within the encampment. "You military now?" he asked with concern.

"Akio, we don't have much time. I need your help. Charlie went missing behind enemy lines. His plane went down outside of Hiroshima. You've got to help me find him. You used to tell me stories about your family that lived in the villages outside of Hiroshima." Akio remained quiet for a moment.

"I know like back of hand," he replied. "I will help you, child. How we get to Japan?" Margaret chuckled.

"I'm going to fly us there, Akio." Akio inhaled deeply then puffed his cheeks letting the air out audible.

"You fly plane? Oh no!" he cried. "I thought you only knew how fix clothes." He laughed hysterically.

Margaret couldn't help but feel anxious as her plans to rescue Charlie began to unfold. Through her many contacts, she was able to retrieve the approximated coordinates where the plane had crashed. She went over every detail with Akio.

"Know crash area...many villages to hide," he said. "If Japanese soldiers are in, villages will be extremely dangerous." Akio was pointing to several isolated sections on the map. "Good chance Charlie alive if stay hidden. Otherwise, will take as prisoner and..." He did not finish. Margaret felt a huge knot in her throat. She realized the mission she was about to begin could be deemed suicidal. But that didn't matter. There was only one way to save Charlie, and that was to go behind enemy lines and bring him home.

Within the next few days, Akio had corresponded with a few of his loyal friends inside his homeland. In the meantime, Margaret eagerly volunteered to fly the supply plane to drop food rations to land troops overseas. This could be the flight she had been waiting for to execute her rescue plans. But even with the help of Akio, Margaret knew she could not attempt the rescue alone. As the two of them looked over her notes, Margaret began to feel a bit defeated. It was then she decided to confide in three of her close comrades. If she could win them over, she just might have a chance. Margaret told her friends about the rescue.

"I can't ask you to do that for me, Lisa," replied Margaret.

"Nonsense; didn't you hear? There's going to be a bill introduced in the United States House of Representatives. It's to give us WASPs military status—but it doesn't look promising. In fact, if it doesn't pass, they're thinking about disbanding the whole lot of us after the war. So, if we can help you in anyway, we'll do it; right, ladies?" Lisa Harris gave the thumbs-up sign to her fellow WASPs. "Besides, it won't be long before someone catches on to the fact that your orders to remove Takahashi from the encampment were completely bogus." The women laughed. It helped ease Margaret's building tension. She felt more confident with her friends' support and eagerness to rescue Charlie.

It took two days to execute the rescue plans. "Okay, I already arranged to be your copilot for the mission. Barbara will be assisting in the drop, and Betty is coming along for the ride," said Lisa.

"You're sure you can slip Akio aboard the plane without anyone noticing?" asked Margaret for the tenth time.

Betty Montgomery rolled her eyes. She adjusted the belt around her thin waist. "I'm telling you, Margaret, quit worrying about Takahashi. If I need to show a little cleavage to distract the male military personnel, well... it may be that those boys get a quick look at the best chest on the coast!" Betty was tall, slim and blond with a knock-out figure. Her beautiful deep blue eyes instantly captivated the yearning hearts of the opposite sex. Male heads turned when Betty walked into a room—especially men in uniforms.

"Barbara, what about the padding inside the crates?" quizzed Margaret.

Barbara Mathieson tried to ignore the repetitive questions. Her dark curls and flashing green eyes gave a care-free look. "Margaret, how many times do I have to repeat myself? You and Takahashi will be just fine. You'll have enough rations for one week. I also packed a compass, map, binoculars, a radio transmitter, and a few other essentials. Remember, you have a week to find Charlie and be back at the designated point of rendezvous," explained Barbara one more time, hoping it would be the last.

"By the way, Barbara, how did you arrange for you, Lisa and Betty to fly the supply plane with me?" queried Margaret.

Barbara smiled, then batted her long black eye lashes. "You seem to forget whose daddy runs this base. What daddy's little girl wants, daddy's little girl gets!" she giggled with delight.

"And Margaret," added Lisa, "if for any reason you think you'll be back before the scheduled time, use the coded transmission sequence I gave you." Margaret exhaled, then briefly closed her eyes. She then glanced around at all her friends.

"I don't know how to thank all of you for what you are about to do for me and Charlie. You're the best friends anyone could ever have in a lifetime." And with that said, and a huge bear hug among them, the four women headed in separate directions as they readied themselves for the impending flight.

The drop was to be made under the cover of night. This would help to conceal their landing behind enemy lines. As the C-56 Lodestar was being loaded with supplies, Betty quickly smuggled Akio Takahashi through the cargo bay door. Margaret nervously paced back and forth across the latrine floor.

"You need to stay focused, Margaret," said Lisa. "Betty knows what she's doing."

"It's done," announced Betty as she burst through the wooden door.

Margaret jumped back with surprise. "How did you do it?" Betty's uniformed shirt was partially unbuttoned. The other women stared at Betty's revealing bosom.

"They never knew what hit them, those poor boys!" she boasted. Barbara shook her head in disbelief.

"Okay, just take a deep breath, and let's get on our way—we have a mission to complete," reported Lisa. The bottom hatch of the C-56 Lodestar had been sealed, and was ready for takeoff. Within minutes, the huge carrier was flying high in the sky, far away from the Los Angeles military airbase, towards the remote villages of Japan.

# Chapter 5

The overseas flight was long and tedious, consuming more than twelve hours in the air. Akio had fallen fast asleep inside the holding compartment. Margaret felt anxious. Her mind kept jumping ahead to the gist of the true mission.

"You realize, Lisa, they will consider me AWOL when I don't report back after this mission."

But Lisa did not respond immediately. Her attention had been diverted to the nasty weather conditions, which were approaching extremely fast. "Margaret, need I remind you that we are technically classified as civilians? Maybe it could be considered a breach of contract or oath, but nothing more than that, my friend. Anyway, it's worth it. I still can't believe the military left Charlie and the others stranded inside enemy lines." The wind was picking up. Lightning flashed across the stormy sky.

"We're running into turbulence; let's get her above this mess!" shouted Lisa.

Margaret pulled back hard on the throttle. Magnificently, the enormous bird responded with ease. It wasn't long before they climbed higher and higher above the heavy, dark clouds. Suddenly, the C-56 Lodestar burst through into the dark night, where thousands of stars sparkled like diamonds in the sky.

"It's so beautiful!" whispered Lisa. Margaret smiled at her friend across the immense cockpit.

"You'll be just fine, Margaret. I have a gut feeling you'll find Charlie without tangling with our adversaries and bring him home safe. Don't be long, okay?" Lisa's eyes glistened. The teary woman choked back her emotions.

"Lisa, if for some reason we don't make it back..." Margaret's voice trailed away.

"I don't want to hear it. You're coming back, Margaret, with Charlie by your side and the rest of the soldiers. Do you understand me?" she ordered. Margaret gave a slight nod. The two women remained quiet, and drifted off into their own private thoughts. Within the hour, the blazing sun came up and stayed.

As the humongous supply plane crossed through the time zone, nightfall once again darkened the peaceful sky.

"Okay, let's drop off the crates and get on with the real reason we're here in the first place," murmured Lisa. Barbara and Betty already arranged the large crates near the back of the cargo door. Lisa gave the signal, and the two women began shoving the supplies from the tail end of the plane. Once the wooden crates hit the air, it took only seconds before the enormous parachutes to deploy. Fifty crates filled with food rations were left behind, floating aimlessly through the air as they made their way down to the drop sight for U.S. soldiers.

"You're up, Margaret; good luck, and I'll see you soon." Lisa smiled. Margaret moved out of her seat and let Betty take over the controls. She stood for a brief moment and stared at her two good friends.

"Get going!" exploded Betty. Margaret swallowed hard. She couldn't say goodbye to her friends. Within seconds she was at the back of the plane. Barbara and Akio were waiting.

"We'll see you in a week, if not sooner, okay? Everything you need is in your backpack." Barbara gave Margaret and Akio each a huge hug. Margaret checked and rechecked her parachute, and that of Akio. He looked nervous as he adjusted his strap.

"Just remember, Akio, you pull the black cord after sixty seconds, and if your chute fails to open, immediately pull the red handle. You'll do fine." Margaret leaned in and kissed him lightly on the cheek. "I can't thank you enough, Akio."

"It's time to go!" shouted Barbara. The cargo door had opened. Instantly, the powerful wind surged into the bay. With nothing left to say, Margaret motioned for Akio to jump. Akio

Takahashi gave a slight bow, and then with finesse, pushed off into a double somersault, then disappeared into the cold night. Barbara gave the thumbs up sign. Within seconds, Margaret followed close behind.

The air was cool and filled with moisture from the heavy clouds. The closing ground approached rapidly as they plummeted anxiously to earth. Akio released his chute, and began a gentle descent near the designated drop zone. In turn, Margaret did the same. The thick green foliage aided them with cover. Minutes later, both tumbled safely to the ground.

"What we do with chutes?" whispered Akio. Margaret motioned to a monstrous bush. He smiled then helped her conceal the evidence of their landing.

"Where are we?" she whispered. Akio pulled out his compass. He remained quiet for a moment. He turned about in a circle.

"This way to village, and remember, do not touch snakes," he said. Akio took the lead. Margaret immediately looked down at her feet.

"I wasn't planning on it," she mumbled to herself. A slight shiver ran up her spine.

"This village might be where they take Charlie," he said. Margaret remained doubtful. She did not say a word.

"Trust me, child. This... is my home!" he said in a low voice. "Follow me!" With that, Akio began to push aside the thick serrated leaves which blocked the path to finding Charlie.

# Chapter 6

The rugged terrain seemed to continue on for miles. The dense jungle made it difficult to travel. Margaret lagged behind. Sweat soaked her clothes.

"See outline of three peaks? Mikura-dake—we're a few miles from Hiroshima," he explained. Margaret closed her burning eyes. They felt like sandpaper.

"Come... Sandankyo Village soon," said Akio. The older man picked up speed.

Margaret's legs felt heavy and drained from the strenuous journey. Her sweaty exposed skin seemed to attract an assortment of insects.

"Akio, how do you know we'll find Charlie at this village?" she asked. She wiped her brow with the back of her hand. Suddenly, Akio stopped dead in his tracks.

"Quiet!" he whispered harshly. Margaret did not move, nor make another sound. Just then, an entanglement of strange voices emerged less than fifty feet away. Akio gently pressed his hand on her shoulder. Immediately, they dropped silently to the patchy ground. The unknown assailants drew near.

"Zwei Amerikaner waren getupft," said a German officer.

"Sie sind spone ud gefunden warden muss," replied another.

"Sie dürfen nicht infiltrieren unsbre Abwehr! Verstehen Sie unter?" shouted the officer.

"Ja," bellowed the guard.

"Was habensie wollen mich mit ihnen zu tun, wenn ich sie gefunden?" the German asked.

"Werden wir die guten Artzt ihnen Folter, umdie informationen, die wir benötigen sie dann zuden Schweimer!" Both men began to laugh hysterically. Margaret's heart pounded in her ears

Thankfully, neither one of them had any idea they had just past the rescue duo hidden within the dense underbrush. As their voices faded in the distance, the two of them began to relax. Margaret could feel the clammy beads of moisture drip down the center of her back.

"What did they say?" she whispered.

"I could understand most of what they said. Let me translate…the Germans know of Americans landing. They think we are spies. When they catch us, they are going to torture us then feed our remains to the pigs." Margaret forced a weak smile—it didn't sound promising at all.

Akio was not disturbed by the crude conversation between the two German soldiers. "Not good, though! No like pigs!" added Akio.

"I guess Hitler must feel a bit threatened and intimidated, now that the tides have turned, and the Americans gained control over the southern portion of the Solomon Islands; that would account for the German military here in Japan. Maybe the Fuhrer thinks the Japanese need a little bit of help, so he sent in reinforcements."

Akio shrugged his shoulders. "Hitler nothing but trouble--Japanese can hold own ground--has done so for centuries," he commented with pride. "We must keep moving to village before daylight comes."

Margaret nodded in agreement. The two of them forged ahead with determination. Sometimes the jungle became so immensely dense, that Margaret felt as if it was choking the life right out of her.

"Taking too much time to reach village. Rest here for moment," said Akio. "I make easier for you." Akio pulled out the machete he had slipped inside the drop bag. Margaret's eyes opened wide. Raising it high above his head, he swung down with precision, cutting the huge leaves and thick foliage. Seconds later, he disappeared, leaving a small path behind. Margaret's head began to throb. The intense heat and claustrophobic conditions weighted on her depleting energy. Suddenly, she heard a hissing sound. She quickly turned around in circles. She dared not to call out to Akio, fearing the enemy might hear her cry for help. The penetrating sound came again, but this time closer. It was then she realized the intruder was up above. There, hanging from a tree branch, was an enormous black and brown snake. Margaret froze. Inch by inch, the venomous reptile eased its slippery body closer and closer to Margaret's frigid body, his slimy tongue darting in and out. Margaret's eyes became fixated on this lethal creature. Her breathing quickened. The jungle serpent sensed his fearful victim and lunged with accuracy. Margaret's voice sprang up her throat in protest.

"No!" she screamed. But as Margaret raised her arms in defense, she was unexpectedly knocked to the ground. With one precise swipe, Akio's machete founds its way, cutting the head right off the viper. It's long, thin body and separated head lay dead on the ground.

Akio looked down at Margaret. "Told you look out for snakes," he mumbled.

Margaret instantly regained her posture. "I thought... I thought you were kidding," she said.

Akio shook his head side to side. "No kid about snake. Come, I made path easier to walk to village." Margaret hurried right behind Akio. It wasn't long before they reached the treacherous mountain road which led up the ascending slope to the village of Sandankyo.

Sandankyo was no more than the size of a city block. The houses had been elevated and constructed from wild bamboo and pine trees. A small bridge crossed over a narrow stream, which jagged its way straight through its center. A few of the villagers were busy carrying buckets of fresh water to their homes, and paid little attention to the strangers. In fact, several of them pretended as if Margaret and Akio did not exist.

"Where is everyone?" asked Margaret. "Surely there must be more villagers?" They cautiously walked along the main road.

"Japanese men working on runway," said Akio.

"I thought the runway was abandoned," responded Margaret. Her thoughts jumped to her friends.

"No one use in long time, until now," he said.

Margaret felt a rush of panic. "Akio, do you realize that's the airstrip Lisa and the others are planning to use for our rescue?" Akio's eye sprung open.

"No use now! Must find other way to get back!" he said with a frightened look in his eyes. "You must somehow get word to your friends."

Suddenly, Margaret felt struck down. Even if they did find Charlie, how would they be able to escape the Germans and make it safely back to the United States?

"There," he said pointing. Margaret had learned that a kura-zukuri-style structure housed only the wealthy in Japan.

"It's actually quite beautiful... do you know the person who lives here?" asked Margaret. Akio looked up at the slim doorway. He nodded his head slowly.

"Akio lives here," he mumbled. Margaret did not move. Akio started to climb the bamboo ladder up to the entrance. "Come," he said. Margaret followed close behind. Akio carefully slid the thatched door open and stepped inside. Within seconds, he took off his shoes and quietly placed them on a woven straw mat.

"Shoes off, please," he whispered. Margaret immediately yanked at her dirty boots. A long hallway ran through the middle of the house, dividing rooms on each side, covered with thin sliding doors. As Margaret and Akio cautiously moved along, Akio kept a watchful eye.

"Where's your family? Doesn't look like anyone is here," commented Margaret. By now, she was on her tiptoes, even though the house seemed to be deserted.

"In here," commanded Akio. He slid open the last door. A square, flat table sat inches above the ground, covered in grimy dust. An enormous pillow, which had been purposely thrown against the streaked wall, was caked with dried blood.

"What does that mean, Akio?" murmured Margaret.

Hurriedly, Akio rushed in and shoved the table to one side. Within seconds, he had removed two planks from the wooden floor. Without hesitation, he pulled out the tattered bag. Surprisingly enough, there was a message.

"Who's it from and what does it say?" Margaret persisted.

"Charlie taken to Buddhist temple in hills," he mumbled. Margaret watched Akio's face. His eyes went blank for a moment.

"What is it, Akio?" she asked. The paper slipped from his hands, then silently fell to the floor.

"Charlie hurt. We must go now; soldiers will come here to find us." Margaret nodded in agreement. The two of them made a mad dash to the front door.

"Look—soldiers!" cried Akio. Margaret grabbed her boots and followed Akio outside.

"Where's this temple they're holding Charlie?" she asked. Akio seemed miles away.

"Akio! Take me to Charlie, now!" shouted Margaret. Margaret's words snagged Akio back to the present.

"Up this way" he said, pointing. Without any further invitation, Akio and Margaret began to climb the rugged and steep hillside, hiding their whereabouts from the impending Nazi troops that stormed the peaceful village.

# Chapter 7

The night breeze came as a relief to her sweating body. Margaret's muscles ached with objection as she arduously climbed the treacherous incline. Her sweaty grip slipped several times sending pieces of rock below. Finally, Aiko reached down to take Margaret's blistered hand.

"Rest here for night." The remote rocky plateau remained hidden against the hillside. Akio pulled out a small fleece blanket from his knapsack, and wrapped it around his tiny shoulders. He eagerly lay down upon the bumpy ground. Within a matter of minutes, he was fast asleep. Margaret felt extremely exhausted, but could not sleep. The ground was hard and uncomfortable. She sat upright and pulled her wrap tighter. By now, the temperature had dropped drastically as the night deepened. Margaret gazed at the star-filled sky above. She wondered if she would ever see Charlie alive again. Her mind quickly wandered to the blood stained pillow in Akio's home. She closed her heavy eyes. A single tear skirted down her dirty cheek. Then, finally, fatigue took control. Margaret slipped into a restless slumber.

"We must move, my child." Akio gently nudged Margaret. Her eyes felt like sand paper. She blinked several times to adjust to the blinding sunlight.

"Look!" said Akio. He gestured to their surroundings. The scenery was breathtaking. Rolling waves of grassy fields seemed endless. Yellow and red gypsy flowers spotted the countryside. Her back was sore from sleeping against the hard rock. Akio was busily eating his ration of breakfast. Margaret's stomach rumbled from hunger.

"Eat now; you need strength to go see Charlie," he said with a smile. Margaret eagerly ate then drank from the canteen filled with fresh water.

"Mile or two; must make temple by midday," said Akio pointing straight ahead.

"I'm ready when you are," Margaret chimed in. Akio and Margaret walked in silence for quite awhile. Finally, Margaret's suspicions needed some kind of definite confirmation.

"Akio, do you think Charlie is still alive?" she asked. Akio did not respond right away. Instead, his pace slowed a bit so they could walk side by side.

"You need to find Charlie, soon," he said. Margaret's spirits were crushed by his open-ended honesty.

"The blood... back at the house... do you think it was Charlie's?" she asked hesitantly.

Akio abruptly stopped. His eyes were filled with concern. "You like daughter to me, my child. I cannot lie. Charlie must be found soon." Akio then turned and quickened his pace.

Margaret tried desperately to hold back her tears. *Was she too late? Was Charlie dying? Is that why he had been taken to the monastery?* Horrible images flashed through her mind.

"Up there... path to temple," said Akio.

Once again, they were at the bottom of a slight incline. Margaret's hands still burned from the torn blisters across her throbbing palms. The dirt road was covered with sharp rocks, but the climb seemed much easier to tackle this time. Margaret's perseverance pushed ahead and stayed strong. It wasn't long before they reached the temple.

The Eiheiji Monastery was a magnificent stone structure. Carved out of granite rock, the entrance gate to the temple grounds stood at least two stories tall. Twelve red, round wooden columns with black-painted bases held the immense irimoya-style roof.

"It has been many years since Akio studied inside Eiheiji. Come, child," uttered Akio.

Margaret and Akio passed through the enormous structure and followed the stone-cut pathway. There, nestled amongst a beautifully landscaped garden, dotted with rare species of Japanese trees, was the kondo—the main hall. This illustrious building had been adorned with Buddha carvings and gilded twin dragons. To the far right stood an impressive bell tower which held a forty-eight-ton bronze bell, and to the left was the most exquisite building of them all: a three-level pagoda. Its solid stone platform was shaped in the form of a square. On each side were wooden stairs which lead to a door that housed many Buddha relics.

"Akio!" called a voice from inside. Instantly, the two of them stopped. Suddenly, Akio sprang forward. The large wooden doors opened wide. There stood a short Japanese monk. His bald head shined in the sunlight.

"Shuji!" cried Akio. Immediately, both men bowed respectfully.

"What took so long?" asked the Japanese man in broken English.

Akio smiled and patted Shuji on the shoulder. "My friend Shuji Akita. This is Margaret Whitmore, American." Akio's introductions were brief.

Shuji Akita gave Margaret a slight bow. The flowing brown robe touched the ground. Happiness filled his round face.

"Nice to meet you, Mr. Akita," she said politely.

"You American woman, aaah," he said while shaking his head up and down. "Come. Akihiko and Hiroki inside."

Akio grabbed Margaret's hand and led her into the main area. The large room was spectacular. Oriental sculptures and statues decorated the immense hall.

"Safe in tunnels, follow please!" said Shuji. The slippery stone stairway led down into a dark, dingy, sublevel underground.

"Come…warmer by fire," said Shuji. Margaret and Akio followed him into the manmade cave. Instantly, waves of warmth radiated from the roaring blaze.

"Akihiko, Hiroki! Many years!" cried Akio. He bowed quickly to each one of them.

Margaret watched in delighted at Akio's reunion with his long time friends, Akihiko Nogi and Hiroki Isoda. As the four men chattered in Japanese, Margaret's attention slowly turned to the military cot sitting near the burning fireplace. Suddenly, appearing from another entrance, limped a tall uniformed man, leaning on a bamboo stick. His head hung low as he painfully made his way back to the flat mattress. Margaret watched him carefully, consumed with hope. *Could this be her fiancé? Wounded, but alive?*

"Charlie?" she questioned in disbelief. "Is that you?"

The soldier abruptly stopped and remained staring at the graveled floor. Shadows danced across his face from the flaming fire. Without waiting for any type of confirmation, she dashed eagerly to his side.

"Charlie…" she whispered. Margaret held on to the last sliver of hope.

The fatigued soldier gently laid his long hand upon her sagging shoulder. "Margaret, I thought I lost you forever, my love," he sobbed. The wounded man pulled her tight against his trembling body. She kissed his tear-stained face over and over again. Charlie Livingston wept with joy. The four Japanese men watched in amazement.

"Charlie hurt, not dead!" announced Akio.

"I've dreamt about you day and night," Charlie cried. "I thought… I thought I would never see you again, my angel."

Margaret pressed her lips eagerly upon his. "I never gave up, Charlie. I would have kept searching, even if it took me the rest of my life to find you," she whispered.

Charlie's smile spread from ear to ear. Then something caught his eye—it was Margaret's uniform. "What's this?" he asked, completely baffled. He released his grip and stumbled back a step or two. He gazed at her adoringly.

"It was the only way to find you… I'm a WASP!" she proclaimed. He slowly shook his head with approval.

"Wait a minute; *you* know how to fly a plane?"

"And jump with parachute from plane!" added Akio. Margaret began to laugh.

"Where are the others?" Charlie looked about.

"There are no others, Charlie. It's only Akio and I who dared to find you, my love." Charlie pulled her close once again.

"Oh Charlie, I have so much to tell you. I'll explain everything later." Suddenly, Margaret glanced around the cave. "Charlie, where are the other soldiers who were with you on the plane? The General told me that four of you survived the crash." She looked deep within his sorrowful eyes.

Charlie's eyes moistened. "They… they didn't make it, Margaret. I was badly hurt, and I didn't want to lessen their chance of survival, so I told them to leave me behind. They… they walked right into an ambush. The Nazis cut them down like weeds. I hid until it was all over with, and then managed to get myself to the village. Shuji helped me escape to the monastery. If only I could have…" Charlie could no longer stand. His legs were weak. Sweat lined his brow. He plopped down onto the worn mattress.

Margaret could see that Charlie blamed himself for the deaths of his comrades. "Charlie, there was nothing you could do. Look at yourself, you can barely walk as it is, and you're burning up with fever! Charlie, you must listen to me now. We need to leave as soon as possible. The Nazis know we're here," she said with teary eyes. All four Japanese men rambled on in their own language.

"Other monks escaped through tunnels. We must, too," explained Hiroki.

"Tunnel lead to Inland Sea, then can signal U.S. ship," added Shuji.

Suddenly, Margaret remembered her friends back home. "Wait! I must find a radio. The landing strip to bring us home was supposed to be deserted, but now, it has been overrun by the Germans. I've got to warn my friends!" Worried lines tugged across her face.

Akio led Margaret back upstairs into a room the size of a closet. Inside sat a Navy model TCS-8 transmitter and receiver. Margaret was amazed by this advance type of military communication system housed inside a Japanese monastery.

"Where did you get this? If I'm not mistaken, you can only find something this technical on a Navy ship!" she said.

"You know how to use?" asked Akio.

"Yes, believe it or not, it was part of my training." She quickly examined the front panel of the transmitter. With a little luck, it just might work.

"Was in Japanese military long ago…taken from American submarine." A tiny grin crawled across his face. Margaret was taken aback by Akio's honesty.

"We'll talk about this later, but for now I need to get a message out before it's too late!" Margaret set the frequencies Betty had written down for her. Within minutes, she was speaking with Lisa, and warned her friend of the waiting disaster.

"How will you return to the states, over?" asked Lisa.

Margaret remained silent for a brief moment. "I'm not sure yet. But I have to sign off for now. The Germans are getting closer, over and out," said Margaret.

"Good luck, Margaret." The radio went dead, and static filled the empty air.

"We must go now," insisted Akio. The two of them rushed back to join the others.

"Long way to Inland Sea; must go before enemy find us," insisted Shuji. As the small group quickly gathered a few supplies, the Nazis had already discovered the monastery, and were breaching the exterior grounds.

"Es gibt tunnel unter. Amerikaner müssen es," stated the Inspekteur des Heeres. Several soldiers stood at attention and waited patiently for their orders.

"Das kloster und tunnels!" he shouted with anger. The firing coordinates were immediately relayed to the huge German tank. Within seconds, it veered its ugly head and aimed directly for the architectural landmark filled with irreplaceable Japanese history. The first deafening blast hit its mark, crumbling the two-story entrance to the ground. Then, without hesitation or regret, an order was given to demolish the two-hundred-year-old Japanese monastery. Clouds of dust and smoke filled the air. The magnificent structure instantly collapsed from the continuous bombardment of heavy mortar shells. The underground tunnels shook, then shifted from the intense impact.

"They found us!" shouted Charlie. Instantly, he held onto Margaret. They hurriedly made their escape far from the wrath of the German onslaught. Akio briefly looked back as the passageway behind caved in.

"Nothing back there, Akio, instead must look forward. Friends need help," cried Shuji.

"Move!" yelled Hiroki. Without hesitation, the group began to run, fearing for their lives. Dirt and rubble filtered through the massive cracks emanating from the constant pounding. As the tremors began to recede, Charlie and Margaret slowed their pace to catch their breath.

"I can't believe you risked your life to come find me," whispered Charlie. He gazed into her beautiful brown eyes. Suddenly, he leaned in and kissed her hungrily on her dirt-stained lips. Margaret could not resist his magical touch, and held on to this desperate moment in time.

"I love you, Charlie. I've loved you since that first day I saw you at the cleaners," she murmured.

Akio smiled, then mumbled something in Japanese to his friends. Within moments, they were all laughing.

"What's so funny?" asked Margaret. She darted her eyes between the four chuckling men.

"I told them how child hid in clothes; so much for love!" he said. Charlie too began to laugh as he remembered that eventful day. Margaret could not conceal her amusement, and produced a sizable grin. After a few minutes of relaxing, it was time to move on.

"How much farther?" asked Charlie. His limp had become more noticeable from the incessant swelling of his leg. The massive gash from the plane crash had become severely infected. Green pus oozed freely.

"Must find leaves of dokudami plant, or will have to cut off leg to stop gangrene from spreading," said Akio. Margaret's face was contorted with worry.

"What is dokudami? Is that some kind of natural antibiotic?" she asked.

"It's a Japanese medicinal plant," said Charlie. He winced in pain. "After the leaves of the plant are orally ingested, it becomes a blood detoxifier. Within minutes, it completely breaks down within your system, and becomes one of the most powerful antibacterial agents found on the planet. You could almost say the results are… miraculous."

"Where can we find this plant, Akio?" she asked. Charlie was failing fast. She knew if they didn't find the dokudami plant soon, Charlie was sure to die.

"Must make it to Inland Sea soon; there we look for dokudami plant. Hidden secret, only Japanese know of its power." Akio gestured to keep moving.

Hiroko was several yards ahead, when suddenly he rushed back, out of breath. "I hear voices," he said. Akio immediately withdrew a Luger pistol from under his long plaid shirt. Margaret was stunned.

"Where did you get that gun?" she asked.

"Learned much in Japanese army." He silently opened his knapsack. The other three Japanese monks declined the offer of keeping a weapon.

"Here, take this, Margaret—you may need it by the time we get through all of this." Charlie held out a revolver. Margaret took a deep breath and grabbed the handle of the weapon. The strange voices grew near.

"Hide in wall!" whispered Akio. Quickly, the group scattered and concealed themselves within the folds of the earth. The German soldiers were few. They slowly walked by, chatting amongst each other, oblivious to the fact they had just passed the enemy.

"Warum sind wir hier?" asked the young Nazi.

"Suche nach affen!" exclaimed the officer. Both men burst out laughing. Margaret did not move. But it was within that split second one of the Germans must have noticed something odd. Suddenly, he stopped and withdrew his weapon.

"Wer geht es?" shouts the Nazi.

"Ich werede schleben!" yells the other soldier.

Then, without rendering a single word, Akio and Charlie opened fire. Ear-shattering sounds from the exploding bullets echoed inside Margaret's head. The deadly confrontation lasted no more than a minute. Hiroki stood over the two dead Nazi soldiers. Their flowing blood soaked the ground beneath them.

"We must go!" shouted Akihiko.

Margaret's hand trembled. She too, without knowing, had fired upon them, not giving her enemy the slightest chance to retaliate.

"Are you alright, my dear?" asked Charlie. They purposely lagged behind the others.

"Charlie, I can't bear the thought of... I just want to get back to the States as soon as possible," she said. Margaret shoved the gun inside her waistband.

Charlie's strength continued to falter. His limp became more prominent, and with it the pain. His foot dragged along the dirt-covered trail.

"Akio!" shouted Margaret. Akio immediately stopped and came back to help Charlie. By now, he was hanging desperately onto Margaret's shoulders for support.

"I'm sorry, my good man, but it seems I feel a bit under the weather." Charlie fainted and dropped to the earth.

"Charlie!" cried Margaret.

Shuji rushed to his side. "Needs dokudami plant soon, or will die," he said while examining Charlie's gaping wound.

"End of tunnel up ahead!" exclaimed Hiroki. The two men lifted Charlie and hurriedly began to drag his body outside the tunnel. The night had begun to pass. Shreds of early light appeared above the horizon. The sun felt warm through the cool air.

"Find dokudami plant near water," said Hiroki. Akio and Shuji gently laid Charlie down upon the damp field.

"Margaret stay with Charlie, will bring back leaves of dokudami plant," insisted Akio.

Margaret ripped a piece of sleeve from her blouse, and dabbed at Charlie's sweating forehead. The raging fever climbed even higher. The infection continued to spread throughout his body. Finally, Akio returned with the plant.

"Wake Charlie; must eat leaves." Akio slapped Charlie's face with force. Charlie blinked several times.

"Who hit me?"

"Eat!" commanded Hiroki. He slowly shoved two dokudami leaves inside his mouth. Charlie gagged from the extreme bitterness of the plant. But after a couple of tries, he was able to chew the lifesaving flower.

"More!" ordered Shuji. Margaret snatched the leaves and shoved them into his mouth. Once again, revulsion veered its ugly head. Akio handed Margaret the canteen full of water. Charlie forcefully washed down the life-saving medicine.

"Now what?" asked Margaret. Charlie laid back.

"We wait," said Akio. Margaret watched with hope. She held him in her arms. Charlie, once again, closed his tired eyes.

"Maybe he didn't eat enough leaves!" said Margaret. She dabbed his sweated brow. Minutes turned to almost an hour. The small group sat together waiting. Then suddenly, Akio jumped up and looked around.

"We are not safe here; must carry Charlie. Must move!" exclaimed Akio.

Just then, Charlie's eyes fluttered open. "Look!" said Akio.

"Charlie! How do you feel?" asked Margaret. He gazed up at Margaret and smiled.

"You look beautiful, my love!" The Japanese men burst out laughing.

"He much better...he sees only woman!" chuckled Hiroki. "But no time for love talk now. We must move like Akio said." As the dokudami plant took hold of Charlie's immune system, his strength slowly returned. It wasn't long before Charlie finally was able to stand on his own.

Let's go home!" he replied with gusto. By now, the sun's rays shined bright. The small group made their way to the port of the Inland Sea. A few Japanese fishing boats still lingered in its harbor. Hiroki and Akihiko were busily speaking to one of the local villagers.

"He agreed to take us to other side where ship leaving soon to cross Pacific Ocean. We must go now. Nazis moving in on foot, still searching for us," said Hiroki.

Akio, his friends, Margaret, and Charlie loaded themselves onto the old, flat fishing boat. The smooth dark water parted with ease as they skirted across the Inland Sea. Margaret had finally begun to relax and think about the return trip home. Charlie seemed content with his arm about her waist and his head against her mussed-up hair.

"They left you for dead, Charlie," she murmured. Charlie did not respond right away. He gazed into her loving eyes before he spoke.

"I knew what my chances were when I volunteered for the mission, Margaret. Believe me when I tell you how torn I felt between my everlasting love for you and my loyalty to my country." He pulled her close and whispered into her ear. "I promise never to leave you again, my dearest." And then he kissed her gently on the lips.

She caressed his dirty face with her trembling hand. "Please, Charlie, don't make a promise you cannot keep," she sobbed.

"Oh, my love, from this day on, I will be forever by your side." Margaret held on tight, never to let go.

"Aaaah, feeling better?" asked Shuji. Margaret blushed instantly. Charlie reluctantly released her. The four Japanese comrades smiled and began to converse amongst themselves.

Within thirty minutes they were all standing on the dock next to the anchored vessel Takanami. Captain Kato Tadao was in deep conversation with Akio. Crew and civilians alike barely glanced in the direction of the two out-of-place Americans. After a few minutes of chatting, Captain Tadao quickly bowed, then headed up the gangplank toward the deck.

"Hide in cargo hole; when close to U.S. ship, will drop lifeboat. Must leave now, Takanami soon to go." Akio, Margaret, and Charlie made their way to the stern of the enormous ship.

"Go, now, and good luck!" Akio stepped back away from Margaret.

"Wait! What are you doing, Akio? You and your friends must come back with us to the States!" she cried. Panic gripped her inside at the horrible thought of leaving Akio behind to face the devastating wrath of the Nazis.

"My home is here, my child." Without saying another word, Akio spun on his heel and quickly disappeared within the mass of confusion moving about the dock.

"Thank you, Akio, and to your friends, too!" called out Charlie. Margaret stood frozen in her tracks. "Margaret, the ship will be leaving soon, and we must find a place to hide, my dear."

"Akio... saved our lives, Charlie," she whispered. The sadness of leaving her friend behind overwhelmed her.

"Margaret, please, if we don't board soon, all of his efforts will have been in vain," coaxed Charlie. He gently took her hand and guided her in the back end of the ship. They wandered through the tall stacks of crates until finding a concealed spot to hide.

"Do you think we will ever see Akio again?" asked Margaret in a low tone. She huddled close against Charlie's warm chest. He stifled a huge yawn.

"In all honesty, Margaret, no; I think Akio has found his final resting place here within his friends and homeland of Japan." Charlie pulled Margaret close and began to doze into a peaceful sleep.

Margaret could not help but feel sad. The woes of war went way beyond anything she could have ever imagined. As she glanced up at Charlie resting, she realized it had been a miracle he had survived the horrific ordeal. A tiny smile formed across her thin lips. Then, without any warning, a searing pain shot through her head. The intense throbbing careened her into a fit of misery. Before her mind could take control, blackness snatched away her perception of reality.

"Ohhh...my head!" wailed Margaret. The old woman rolled from side-to-side on the dirty floor. Muscles ached through her decrepit body. A huge lump swelled through her thin grey hair. Within seconds, her damp eyes flittered open. "Where am I?" she thought. She could see the photo of her two children staring down at her. "Where's my Charlie?" she shouted. Lying next to her, was the aged photograph covered with shattered glass.

"No! No! It can't be! I was young...I was with Charlie! No! No! I want to go back...back to Charlie!" she cried out in protest. Tears of anguish ran freely down her dust-covered cheeks. The painful memories were all that were left to haunt her. With tremendous effort, she brought herself to kneel then grasp the thick metal walker. Her movements were slow and mechanical.

"Where are my children when I need them the most? All those happy years—the four of us—a family. Where did those wonderful years go?" A rush of tears flooded her wrinkled face.

She turned the key in the weathered lock. The door creaked open. Maggie Livingston hated to see her mother living in such a rundown place. But her mother was stubborn, threatening to change the locks so neither Maggie nor her brother Chuck could enter without their mother's consent.

"Mom!" shouted Maggie. She rushed to her aging mother's side. It was then she saw the shattered photo on the floor. "Are you hurt?"

Margaret pulled away from her daughter. She didn't understand why her children had deserted their mother long ago.

"Why are you here?" asked Margaret. Maggie placed her hands on her hips.

"What do you mean? You know I come here every other day and Chuck in between."

Margaret's mind tried to sort through the clouded images in her mind. "Chuck?" she said in a low tone.

"Yes, Mother, Chuck. Your son. Look, Mom, maybe you shouldn't be alone. There's this really nice place—Manor Care. There's all kinds of things to do, you know, like playing cards, watching movies, activities to keep your mind sharp. Chuck says it's one of the best." Maggie knew her words were not heard. Margaret stood staring down at the aged photo amongst the shards of glass.

"Will you at least think about it, Mom? Please say you will." Maggie grabbed the photo from the floor and placed it back on the dresser. "I'll get you a new frame for your picture." Without hesitation, Maggie grabbed the broom and dustpan to clean up the slivery mess.

Margaret eased herself down on the bed. She stared at the strange woman sweeping.

"Who are you, and what are you doing in my home?" she demanded.

Maggie stopped. Tears swelled in her eyes. "Mom, it's me, Maggie…your daughter. Remember?"

Margaret's head ached. She closed her weary eyes. "I don't have a daughter," she said.

Maggie let out a huge sigh. "Yes, Mom, you do have a daughter. And that daughter is me—Maggie Livingston. You also have a son, Chuck. Your husband's name was Charlie—our father. Mom, do you remember now?" pleaded Maggie.

Margaret's mind was in a whirl. People's faces, names she did not recognize except for one—Charlie. "Charlie is my husband!" cried Margaret.

Maggie set aside the broom and sat down on the bed next to her ailing mother. "Yes, Mom, Charlie *was* your husband. But he's gone now. Gone for quite awhile." Maggie tried to hold the old woman's hands.

"No! Get away from me! You don't know what you're talking about!" Margaret yanked her hands from her daughter's grip.

Tears fell down Maggie's young face. "It's okay, Mom, I know it's hard for you. But Chuck and I are going to do the best thing we can for you. And that is by moving you to Manor Care. You'll get the help and support you physically and mentally need right now."

Suddenly, visions of her daughter raced inside Margaret's head. "Maggie, my dear. It's so good to see you!" Margaret leaned over to Maggie and placed a huge kiss on her cheek. "Why are you crying, dear?"

Maggie wiped the tears with the back of her hand. "Nothing, Mom. I'm fine. Let me finish cleaning up this mess before I go get you some groceries." Maggie stood up and finished the job. Minutes later, Margaret's daughter was gone. Once again, Margaret looked at the broken picture on her dresser.

"Charlie, how could you leave me all alone? You promised me, you promised!" she sobbed. Once again, Margaret's failing mind surged with memories of her husband. But Margaret's will to live had vanished just like the dreams of her beloved Charlie. As Margaret cursed at her pitiful existence, a loud knock came from her front door. Startled by this unexpected intrusion, Margaret forced her mind to focus.

"Now, who could that be?" she whimpered. Again, it came, but this time even louder and much harder. Margaret hesitated, then pushed the walker to the splintered door.

"Who is it?" she called out. Margaret leaned in close. A rush of cold air found its way through the cracks. Shivers ran down her spine.

"Who is it, I say?" A strange silence filled the air. And then came yet another huge thud. This time the entire doorway rattled with urgency. Margaret backed away. Fear building as she reached her shaky hand to unlatch the lock. Without hesitation, she turned the tarnished knob. Suddenly, a warm breeze filled with peace and serenity filled her body.

"Charlie, is that you?" she whispered. For a brief moment, Margaret gazed at the familiar face.

"Margaret, my dear, I've been waiting for you!" he said. The handsome pilot in his olive-drab uniform smiled. He held out his long slender hand to Margaret. Heavenly rays of light radiated from behind.

"Don't be afraid, Margaret. Come with me so we can be together for all eternity!"

"Charlie... you're so young!" her voice edged with disbelief.

"And so are you, Margaret, my love." As his glowing hand touched hers, Margaret's heart skipped a beat. Then, miraculously within a flash of a light, a pure and heavenly essence consumed her inner soul, releasing her tormented body and spirit.

"Charlie, I'm young again, too!" With one swift movement, his loving arms wrapped about her delicate waist.

"And so we shall stay this way, forever…"

MIX

Papier | Fördert
gute Waldnutzung

FSC® C083411

Zeitfracht Medien GmbH
Ferdinand-Jühlke-Straße 7
99095 Erfurt, Deutschland
produktsicherheit@kolibri360.de

Druck:
CPI Druckdienstleistungen GmbH
im Auftrag der
Zeitfracht Medien GmbH
Ein Unternehmen der Zeitfracht - Gruppe
Ferdinand-Jühlke-Str. 7
99095 Erfurt